Contents

Heroes

by

Anne Perry

First published in 2007 in Great Britain by
Barrington Stoke Ltd
18 Walker St, Edinburgh EH3 7LP

www.barringtonstoke.co.uk

ISBN: 978-1-84299-510-5

Printed in Great Britain by Bell & Bain Ltd

Barrington Stoke acknowledges subsidy from the Scottish
Arts Council towards the publication of this volume

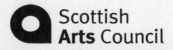

Scottish
Arts Council

A Note from the Author

I wrote 'Heroes' because my mother's father, who was called Joseph Reavley, was a chaplain in the trenches during the First World War. I never knew him but I often heard stories about him from my mother. She said that I was like him in many ways.

I chose the setting of the front line in the war because it offered men a chance to be very brave and also gave them some very hard moral choices. There was no escape for anyone.

Chapter 1

Night in the Dugout

Nights were always the hardest, and in winter they lasted from dusk, at about 4pm, until dawn at eight the next morning. Sometimes star shells lit the sky, showing the black zigzags of the trenches stretching to left and right as far as the eye could see. It was said that now they went right across France and Belgium, all the way from the Alps to the Channel. But Joseph Reavley was only concerned with this short stretch of the Ypres Salient.

In the gloom near him someone coughed, a deep, hacking sound coming from down in the chest. Joseph was in the support line, the farthest from the front, the most complex of the three rows of trenches. Here were the kitchens, the latrines, the stores and the heavy guns. Fifteen-foot shafts led to caves which were about five paces wide, and high enough for most men to stand upright. Joseph made his way along the lines in the half dark now. The wood was slippery under his boots, as his hands felt along the mud walls, held up by timber and wire. There was an awful lot of water. One of the sumps must be blocked.

There was a glow of light ahead and a moment later he was in the dugout. It was warmer here. There were two candles burning and the brazier gave off heat, and a sharp smell of soot. The air was blue with tobacco smoke, and a pile of boots and damp great-coats steamed a little. Two officers sat on canvas chairs talking together. One of them was telling a joke – sick humour – and they both laughed. A gramophone sat silent on a camp table, and a small pile of records of the latest music hall songs were carefully kept away from the damp in a tin box.

"Hello, chaplain," one of them said in a cheerful tone. "How's God these days?"

"Gone home on sick leave," the other said quickly, before Joseph could reply. There was disgust in his voice, but he did not intend any lack of respect. Death was too close here for men to mock faith.

"Have a seat," the first offered, waving towards a third chair. "Morris got it today. Killed outright. That bloody sniper again."

"He's somewhere out there, just about opposite us," the second said grimly. "One of our blighters the other day claimed he'd got 43 for sure."

"I can believe it," Joseph replied, sitting down on the seat he'd been offered. He knew better than most about the numbers of wounded and dead. It was his job to comfort the terrified and the dying, to carry stretchers, often to write letters to the families of the dead men. Sometimes he thought it was harder than doing the actual fighting, but he refused to stay back in the greater safety of the field hospitals and depots. This was where he was most needed.

"Thought about setting up a trench raid," the major said slowly, choosing his words with care and looking at Joseph. "Good for morale. Make it seem as if we were really doing something. But our chances of getting the blighter are pretty small. Only lose a lot of men for nothing. Feel even worse afterwards."

The captain did not add anything. They all knew the morale of the troops was sinking. Losses were high, and the news bad. Word of endless killing seeped through from the Somme and Verdun and all along the line right to the sea. The hardship of the trenches took its toll: the dirt, the cold, and the cruel mix of boredom and terror. The winter of 1916 lay ahead.

"Cigarette?" The major held out his pack to Joseph.

"No, thanks." Joseph refused with a smile. "Got any tea going?"

Chapter 2

Firing Trench

They poured him a mugful, strong and bitter, but hot. He drank it, and half an hour later made his way forward to the open air again and the travel trench.

A star shell exploded high and bright. Without thinking he ducked, keeping his head below the rim. They were about four feet deep, and in order not to provide a target a man had to bend almost double to pass along the lines. There was a rattle of machine gun fire out ahead, and, closer to, a thud as a rat fell into the mud beside the duck-boards.

Other men were moving about close to him. The normal order of things was back-to-front here. Nothing much happened during the day. Trench repair work was done, munitions shifted, weapons cleaned, a little rest taken. Most of the activity was at night, most of the deaths.

"'Lo, chaplain," a voice whispered in the dark. "Say a prayer we get that bloody sniper, will you?"

"Maybe God's a Jerry?" someone called out in the dark.

"Don't be stupid!" a third shouted back in a mocking voice. "Everyone knows God's an Englishman! Didn't they teach you nothing at school?"

There was a burst of laughter. Joseph joined in. He promised to offer up the right prayers and moved on forward.

He had known many of the men all his life. They came from the same town in Cambridgeshire as he did, or the villages round about. They had gone to school together, scrumped apples from the same trees, fished in the same rivers, and walked the same lanes.

It was a little after 6pm when he reached the firing trench. Beyond the sandbag wall, or parapet, lay no-man's-land, with its four or five hundred yards of mud, barbed wire and shell holes. Half a dozen burnt tree stumps looked in the sudden flares like men. Those grey wisps of mist could be fog, or gas.

Funny that in summer this blood-soaked soil, so full of horror, could still bloom with forget-me-nots and other flowers, and most of all with poppies. You would think nothing would ever grow there again.

More star shells went up, lighting the ground, the jagged scars of the trenches black. The men on the fire steps, their rifles at the ready, were lit up for a few, blinding moments. Sniper shots rang out.

Joseph stood still. He knew the terror of the night-watch out beyond the parapet, as they crawled around in the mud. Some of them would be in the tunnels leading out from the trench. Most would be in shell holes, with heavy coils of barbed wire all round. Their job was to check enemy patrols for any odd movement, any signs of greater activity, anything that might give a clue that an attack was being planned.

More star shells lit the sky. It was starting to rain. A crackle of machine-gun fire, and some heavy artillery over to the left.

Then the sharp whine of sniper fire, again and again.

Joseph shuddered. He thought of the men out there, out of sight, and prayed for strength to share their pain, not try to deaden himself to it.

Chapter 3

Rescue?

There were shouts somewhere ahead, heavy shells now, shrapnel exploding. There was a flurry of movement, flares, and a man came sliding over the parapet, shouting for help.

Joseph plunged forward, sliding in the mud, grabbing onto the wooden props to hold himself up. Another flare of light. He saw quite clearly someone he knew well, Captain Holt, lurching towards him, another man on his back, dead weight.

"He's hurt!" Holt gasped. "Pretty badly. One of the night patrol. Panicked. Just about got us all killed." He eased the man down into Joseph's arms and let his rifle slide forward, bayonet covered in an old sock to hide its gleam. His face was distorted in the lantern light, filthy with mud and with a wide streak of blood over the burnt cork with which he'd blackened it, as all night patrol did. His trousers were ripped to pieces.

Others were coming to help. There was still a terrible noise of fire going on, and every now and then a flare.

The man in Joseph's arms did not stir. His body was limp and it was hard to support him. Joseph felt the wetness and the smell of blood. Silently others appeared out of the gloom and took the weight of the body.

"Is he alive?" Holt said in an urgent, shaking voice. "There was a hell of a lot of shot up there." He was almost out of control.

"Don't know," Joseph answered. "We'll get him back to the bunker and see. You've done all you can." He knew how desperate men felt when they risked their lives to save another man and he died. A kind of despair set in. It was a sense of personal failure, almost of guilt for having survived themselves. "Are you hurt?"

"Not much," Holt replied. "Couple of grazes."

"Better have them dressed, before they get poisoned," Joseph advised. His feet slipped on the wet boards and he banged his arm against a jutting post. The whole trench wall was crooked, giving way under the weight of mud. The base had eroded.

The man helping him swore.

The wounded man was hard to carry. The men staggered back along the travel line to the support trench and into the light and shelter of a bunker.

Holt looked awful. Beneath the cork and blood his face was ashen grey. He was soaked with rain and mud and there were dark patches of blood across his back and on his arms.

Someone gave him a cigarette. Back here it was safe to strike a match. He drew in smoke deeply. "Thanks," he muttered, still staring at the wounded man.

Joseph looked down at him now. It was young Ashton. He knew him quite well. He had been at school with his cousin.

The soldier who had helped carry him in let out a cry of dismay, choked in his throat. It was Morton, Ashton's closest friend, and he could see what Joseph now could also see. Ashton was dead, his chest torn open, the blood no longer pumping, and a bullet hole through his head.

Chapter 4

Shame

"I'm sorry," Holt said softly. "I did what I could. I didn't get to him in time. He panicked."

Morton jerked his head up. "Will would never!" The cry was desperate, a burning need to deny a shame too great to be borne. "Not our Will!"

Holt drew himself up stiffly. "I'm sorry," he said in a cracked voice. "It does happen."

"Not with Will Ashton, it don't!" Morton yelled back at him, his eyes blazing, pupils circled with white in the candle-light, his face grey. He had been in the front line two weeks now. This was a long stretch without a break from the constant tension, filth, cold and those dangerous silences followed by ear-splitting noise. He was nineteen.

"You'd better go and get that arm dressed, and your side," Joseph said to Holt. He made his voice firm, as to a child.

Holt glanced again at the body of Ashton, then up at Joseph.

"Don't stand there bleeding," Joseph ordered. "You did all you could. There's nothing else. I'll look after Morton."

"I tried!" Holt repeated. "There's nothing out there but mud and darkness and wire, and bullets coming from all sides." There was a sharp tone of terror under his eggshell-thin

self-control. He had seen too many men die.
"It would make any man lose his nerve."

"Not Will!" Morton said again, his voice
choking off in a sob.

Holt looked at Joseph again, then
staggered out.

Joseph turned to Morton. He had done
this before, too many times, tried to comfort
men who had just seen childhood friends
blown to pieces, or killed by a sniper's bullet.
Dead men could look as if they should still be
alive, perfect except for the small blue hole
through the brain.

There was little to say. Most men found
talk of God had little meaning at that
moment. They were shocked, trying not to
accept the truth, and yet seeing in front of
their eyes all the terrible waste and loss.
Most of the time it was best just to stay with
them, let them speak about the past, what

the friend had been like and the times they had shared. They would talk as if the dead man were only wounded and would be back, at the end of the war, in some world they could only imagine. It could be in England, perhaps on a summer's day with sunlight on the grass, birds singing, a quiet riverbank somewhere, the sound of laughter, and women's voices.

Morton refused to be comforted. He accepted Ashton's death. The stark truth of that was too clear for him to deny. He had seen too many other men he knew killed in the year and a half he had been in Belgium. But he could not, would not accept that Ashton had panicked. He knew what panic out there cost, how many other lives it put at risk. It was the final defeat.

"How am I going to tell his mam?" he begged Joseph. "It'll be all I can do to tell her he's dead! His pa'll never get over it. That proud of him, they were. He's the only boy. Three sisters he had, Mary, Lizzie and Alice.

Thought he was the greatest lad in the world. I can't tell 'em he panicked! He couldn't have, chaplain! He just wouldn't! I'm going to find out what really happened."

Joseph did not know what to say. How could people at home in England even begin to imagine what it was like in the mud and noise out here? But he knew how deep the shame could burn. A lifetime could be destroyed by it.

"Maybe he just lost his sense of direction," Joseph told Morton gently. "He wouldn't be the first."

War changed men. People did panic. Morton knew that, and half his horror was because it could be true. But Joseph didn't say so. "I'll write to his family," he went on. "There's a lot of good to say about him. I could send pages. I'll not need to tell them much about tonight."

"Will you?" Morton was eager. "Thanks ... thanks, chaplain. Can I stay with him ... until they come for him?"

"Yes, of course," Joseph agreed. "I'm going forward anyway. Get yourself a hot cup of tea. See you in an hour or so."

Chapter 5

Another Death

Joseph left Morton squatting on the earth floor beside Ashton's body. He fumbled his way back over the slimy duck-boards towards the travel line, then forward again to the front and the crack of gunfire, with now and then the high flare of a star shell.

He did not see Morton again, but he did not think this was odd. He could have passed twenty men he knew and not known who they were. They were all muffled in great-coats, heads bent as they moved, rattling along the duck-boards. Or they were standing on the fire steps, rifle to shoulder, trying to see something to aim at in the gloom.

Now and again he heard a cough, or the scamper of rats' feet and the splash of rain and mud. He spent a little time with two men swapping jokes, joining in their laughter. It was black humour, self-mocking, but he did not miss the courage in it, or the friendship, the need to release emotion in some sane and human way.

About midnight the rain stopped.

A little after five the night patrol came scrambling through the wire, whispered pass words to the sentries, then came tumbling over the parapet of sandbags down into the trench. They were shivering with cold and relief. One of them had been shot in the arm.

Joseph went back with them to the support line. In one of the dugouts a gramophone was playing a music hall song. Two or three men sang along with it; one of them had a beautiful voice, a soft tenor. It was a light and silly song, but out here it sounded almost like a hymn, a praise of life.

A couple of hours and the day would begin – endless duties of house-keeping, the boring daily rota, but it was better than doing nothing.

There was still a crackle of machine-gun fire every now and then, and the whine of sniper bullets.

Then the crack of a single pistol shot, and, after that, silence for a while.

An hour till dawn.

Joseph was sitting on an upturned ration box when Sergeant Renshaw came into the bunker, pulling the gas curtain aside to peer in.

"Chaplain?"

Joseph looked up. He could see bad news in the man's face.

"I'm afraid Morton got it tonight," he said, coming in and letting the curtain fall again. "Sorry. Don't really know what happened. Found him lying on the duck-boards. Must have got a direct hit as he went over the parapet and have fallen back into the trench. Ashton's death seems to have ... well, he lost his nerve. More or less went over the top all by himself. Suppose he had made his mind up to go and give Fritz a bloody nose, for Ashton's sake. Stupid bastard! Sorry, chaplain."

He did not need to explain himself, or say he was sorry. Joseph knew exactly the fury and grief he felt at such a pointless waste. To this was added a sense of guilt that he had not stopped it. He should have understood that Morton was so close to breaking. He should have seen it. That was his job.

He stood up slowly. "Thanks for telling me, sergeant. Where is he?"

"He's gone, chaplain." Renshaw remained near the doorway. "You can't help him now."

"I know that. I just want to ... I don't know ... tell him I'm sorry. I let him down. I didn't understand he was ... so ..."

"You can't be everybody's keeper," Renshaw said gently. "Too many of us. It's not been a bad night otherwise. Got a trench raid coming off soon. Just wish we could get that damn sniper across the way there."

He scraped a match and lit his cigarette. "But morale's good. That was a brave thing Captain Holt did out there. Pity about Ashton, but that doesn't alter Holt's courage. Poor devil went crazy. Running around like a fool. Would have got the whole patrol killed if Holt hadn't gone after him. Could see them, you know, by the light of the star shells. Couldn't make out who they were at

first, right up there near the last wire. Then
suddenly, as they got close, we saw it was
Holt carrying Ashton on his back. Hell of a
job getting him back. Fell a couple of times.
Reckon that's worth a medal or at least a
mention in dispatches. Cheers the men up, if
they see our officers have got that kind of
spirit."

"Yes ... I'm sure," Joseph agreed. He could
only think of Ashton's white face, and how
desperate Morton was to tell him that Ashton
would never have panicked, and how Ashton's
mother would feel, and the rest of his family.
"I think I'll go and see Morton just the same."

"Right you are," Renshaw said. "If you
must." He shook his head and stood aside for
Joseph to pass.

Chapter 6

Looking for Answers

Morton lay in the support trench just outside the bunker two hundred yards to the west. He looked even younger than he had in life, as if he was asleep. His face was oddly calm, even though it was smeared with mud. Someone had tried to clean most of it off as a mark of respect, so that at least anyone could see who he was. There was a large wound in the left side of his forehead. It was bigger than most sniper wounds. He must have been close to the enemy line. But that was odd.

Renshaw said he got hit going over the parapet.

Joseph stood there as dawn began to break and looked at Morton in the light of a candle from the open bunker curtain. He had been so alive only a few hours ago, so full of anger and loyalty and dismay. What had made him throw his life away in a useless act? Joseph racked his mind for some sign that should have warned him Morton was so close to breaking, but he couldn't see it even now.

There was a cough a few feet away, and the tramp of boots on duck-boards. The men were stood down and were leaving their posts, just one sentry per platoon left. They had returned for breakfast. Joseph felt hungry too.

Now would be the time to ask around and find out what had happened to Morton.

He made his way to the field kitchen. It was packed with men, some standing close to

28

the stoves to catch a bit of their heat, others choosing to sit, though then they were further away. They had survived the night. They were laughing and telling stories, most of them unfit for polite company, but Joseph was too used to this to mind. Now and then someone new would apologise for using such language in front of a chaplain, but most knew he understood only too well.

"Yeah," one replied to Joseph's question, as he chewed a mouthful of bread and jam. "Morton came up and asked me if I saw what happened to Ashton. Very cut up, he was."

"And what did you tell him?" Joseph asked.

The man gulped the mouthful down. "Told him Ashton seemed fine to me when he went over. Just like anyone else, nervy ... but then only a fool isn't scared to go over the top!"

Joseph thanked him and moved on. He needed to know who else was on the patrol.

"Captain Holt," the next man told him, a ring of pride in his voice. Word had got around about Holt's courage. Everyone stood a little taller because of it, felt a little braver, more confident. "We'll pay Fritz back for that," he added. "Next raid – you'll see."

They all cheered at that.

"Who else?" Joseph pressed.

"Seagrove, Noakes, Willis," a thin man replied, standing up. "Want some breakfast, chaplain? Anything you like for nothing – as long as it's bread and jam and half a cup of tea. But you're not choosy, are you? Not one of those fussy eaters who'll only take kippers and toast?"

"What I wouldn't give for a fresh Craster kipper," another sighed, a faraway look in his eyes. "I can smell them in my dreams."

Someone told him in a friendly way to shut up.

Chapter 7

Witnesses

"Went over the top beside me," Willis said when Joseph found him half an hour later. "All blacked up like the rest of us. Seemed OK to me then. Lost him in no-man's-land. Had a hell of a job with the wire. As bloody usual, it wasn't where we'd been told. Got through all right, then Fritz opened up on us. Star shells all over the sky. By the way, Morton came and asked me what happened, too."

He sniffed and then coughed hard. When he had control of himself again he went on. "Then I saw someone outlined against the flares, arms high, like a wild man, running around. He was going towards the German lines, shouting something. Couldn't hear what in the noise. Couldn't really see who it was, either."

Joseph let him talk. It was now broad day-light and beginning to drizzle with rain. Around them men were starting the duties of the day: digging, filling sandbags, carrying ammunition, mending the wire, re-setting duck-boards. Men took an hour's work, an hour's sentry duty, and an hour's rest.

Near them someone was using every curse he knew against the lice. Two more were making a complex plan to hold the water back.

"Of course," Willis went on, "when the Germans saw someone running towards their lines they lit us up like a target, didn't they!

Sniper fire and machine guns all over the place. Even a couple of shells. How none of us got hit I'll never know. Perhaps the row woke God up, and he came back on duty!" He laughed grimly. "Sorry, chaplain. Didn't mean it. I'm just so damn sorry poor Ashton got it. Holt just came out of nowhere and ran after him, stumbling through the mud. If Ashton hadn't got trapped in the wire he'd never have got him."

"Caught in the wire?" Joseph asked. There was something odd here.

"Yeah. Ashton must have run right into the wire, because he stopped sudden, teetering, like, and fell over. We thought he was OK. Lying on the ground like that he would have escaped the hell of a barrage that came over just after that. We all threw ourselves down. He must have been hit anyway."

"What happened then?" asked Joseph. He needed to know. A slow, sick thought was taking shape in his mind.

"When it died down I looked up again, and there was Holt staggering back with poor Ashton across his shoulders. Hell of a job he had carrying him, even though he's bigger than Ashton ... well, taller, anyway. Up to his knees in mud, he was, shot and shell all over, sky lit up like a Christmas tree. Of course we gave him what covering fire we could. Maybe it helped."

He gave another cough. "Reckon he'll be mentioned in dispatches, chaplain? He deserves it." There was respect in his voice, a lift of hope.

Joseph forced himself to reply. "I should think so." The words were stiff.

"Well, if he isn't, the men'll want to know why!" Willis said angrily. "Bloody hero, he is."

Joseph thanked him and went to find Seagrove and Noakes. They told him pretty much the same story.

"You going to have him put forward for a medal?" Noakes asked. "Morton came and we said just the same to him. Odd thing was, he wasn't too keen on the captain getting that medal. He made us tell him over and over again, just what happened."

"That's right," Seagrove nodded, leaning on a sandbag.

"You told him the same?" Joseph asked. "About the wire, and Ashton getting caught in it?"

"Yes, of course. If he hadn't got caught by the legs he'd have gone right on and landed up in Fritz's lap, poor devil."

"Thank you."

"You're welcome, chaplain. You going to write up Captain Holt?"

Joseph did not reply, but turned away, sick at heart.

He did not need to look again, but he trudged all the way back to the field hospital anyway. It would be his job to say the services for both Ashton and Morton. The graves would be already dug.

He bent down to look at Ashton's body again, and checked his trousers carefully. They were stained with mud, but there were no tears in them, no marks of wire. The fabric was perfect.

He stood up.

"I'm sorry," he said softly to the dead man. "Rest in peace." And he turned and walked away.

He went back to where he had left Morton's body, but it had been taken away. Half an hour more took him to where it had now been laid out. He touched the cold hand and looked at the brow. He would ask. He would make sure. But in his mind he already was. He needed time to know what he must do about it.

The men would be going over the top on another trench raid soon. Today morale was high. They had a hero in their number, a man who would risk his own life to bring back a soldier who had lost his nerve and panicked. Led by someone like that, they were as good as Fritz any day. Was one pistol bullet, one family's shame, worth all that?

What were they fighting for anyway? On the one hand the conflict was so very big, and at the same time it was so very small and intimate.

Chapter 8

Captain Holt

He found Captain Holt alone just after dusk, standing on the duck-boards below the parapet, near one of the firing steps.

"Oh, it's you, chaplain. Ready for another night?"

"It'll come, whether I am or not," Joseph replied.

Holt gave a harsh laugh. "That doesn't sound like you. Tired of the firing line, are you? You've been up here a couple of weeks, you should be in turn for a step back any day. Me too, thank God."

Joseph faced forward, peering through the gloom toward no-man's-land and the German lines beyond. He was shaking. He must control himself. This must be done in the silence, before the shooting started up again. Then he might not get away with it.

"Pity about that sniper over there," he remarked. "He's taken out a lot of our men."

"Damn shame," Holt agreed. "Can't get a line on him, though. Keeps his own head well down."

"Oh, yes," Joseph nodded. "We'd never get him from here. It needs a man to go over in the dark and find him."

"Not a good idea, chaplain. He'd not come back. You're not suggesting suicide, are you?"

Joseph chose his words very carefully and kept his voice as calm as he could.

"I wouldn't have put it like that," he replied. "But he's cost us a lot of men. Morton today, you know?"

"Yes ... I heard. Pity."

"Except that it wasn't the sniper, of course. But the men think it was, so it comes to the same thing, as far as morale is concerned."

"Don't know what you mean, chaplain." In the darkness there was a slight pause before Holt replied.

"Wasn't a rifle wound, it was a pistol," Joseph replied. "You can tell the difference, if you're looking for it."

"Then he was a fool to be that close to German lines," Holt said, facing forward over the parapet and the mud. "Lost his nerve, I'm afraid."

"Like Ashton," Joseph said. "Can understand that, up there in no-man's-land, mud everywhere, wire catching hold of you,

40

tearing at you, stopping you from moving. Terrible thing to be caught in the wire with the star shells lighting up the night. Makes you an easy target. Takes a very brave man not to panic, when that happens ... a hero."

Holt did not answer.

There was silence ahead of them, only the dull thump of feet and a squelch of duck-boards in mud behind, and the trickle of water along the bottom of the trench.

"I expect you know what it feels like," Joseph went on. "I notice you have some pretty bad tears in your trousers, even one in your tunic. I expect you haven't had time to mend them yet?"

"I dare say I got caught in a bit of wire out there last night," Holt said stiffly. He moved uneasily from one foot to the other.

"I'm sure you did," Joseph agreed with him. "Ashton didn't. His clothes were muddy, but no wire tears."

There were several moments of silence. A group of men passed by behind them, muttering words of greeting. When they were gone, the darkness closed in again. Someone threw up a star shell and there was a crackle of machine gun fire.

"I wouldn't repeat that, if I were you, chaplain," Holt said at last. "You might give people wrong ideas. And right at the moment morale is high. We need that. We've had a hard time these last few days. We're going over the top in a trench raid soon. Morale is important ... trust. I'm sure you know that, even better than I do. That's your job, isn't it? Morale, looking after men's souls?"

"Yes ... care of men's souls," said Joseph. "That's a good way of putting it. Remember what it is we're fighting for, and that it's worth all that it costs ... even this."

Joseph pointed in the dark to all that surrounded them.

More star shells went up, lighting up the night for a few, blinding moments. Then a greater darkness closed in.

Chapter 9

Heroes

"We need our heroes," Holt said very clearly. "Any man who would tear them down would be very unpopular, even if he said he was doing it in the name of truth, or justice, or whatever was in the reason he gave. He would do a lot of harm, chaplain. I expect you can see that ..."

"Oh, yes," Joseph agreed. "If their hero was shown to be a coward who laid the blame for his panic on another man, and let him be laid in his grave in shame. And if this same hero then committed murder to hide what he'd done, that would destroy the morale of men who are already wretched and worn down by war."

"You are quite right." Holt sounded as if he were smiling. "A very wise man, chaplain. Good of the regiment first. The right sort of loyalty."

"I could prove the murder," Joseph said, choosing his words with care.

"But you won't. Think what it would do to the men."

Joseph turned a little to face the parapet. He stood up onto the fire step and looked forward over the dark expanse of mud and wire.

"We should take that sniper out. That would be a very heroic thing to do. Good thing to try, even if you didn't succeed.

You'd deserve a mention in dispatches for that, possibly a medal."

"But I'd be dead before I got it!" Holt said in bitter tones.

"Possibly. But you might succeed and come back. It would be so daring, Fritz would never expect it," Joseph pointed out.

"Then you do it, chaplain!" Holt said with a sarcastic edge.

"It wouldn't help you, captain. Even if I die, I have written a full account of what I have learned today, to be opened should anything happen to me. On the other hand, if you were to mount such a raid, whether you returned or not, I should destroy what I'd written."

There was silence again, except for the distant crack of sniper fire a thousand yards away, and the drip of mud.

"Do you understand me, Captain Holt?"

Holt turned slowly. A star shell lit his face for an instant. His voice was hoarse.

"You're sending me to my death!"

"I'm letting you be the hero you pretend to be, and the one Ashton really was," Joseph replied. "The hero the men need. Thousands of us have died out here. No one knows how many more there will be. Others will be maimed or blinded. It isn't whether you die or not, it's how well."

A shell exploded a dozen yards from them. Both men ducked, an instant reaction.

Silence again.

Slowly Joseph unbent.

Holt lifted his head. "You're a hard man, chaplain. I misjudged you."

"Care of men's souls, captain," Joseph said softly. "You wanted the men to think you were a hero. Now you're going to justify that, and become one."

Holt stood still, looking towards him in the gloom, then slowly he turned and began to walk away, his feet sliding on the wet duck-boards. Then he climbed up the next fire step, and up over the parapet.

Joseph stood still and prayed.

We hope you enjoyed this book!

Turn the page for a sneak preview of another book in this series:
Dead Brigade by James Lovegrove...

Chapter 1
Kurdistan

A thin wind slid like a ghost between the mountain peaks. Sleet seeped down from a grey sky. The cold wet flakes pattered into the soldiers' faces, making their eyes sting. The silence all around was vast. That silence must have existed millions of years ago, before the human race appeared. Every footstep the soldiers made sounded as loud as a shout.

There were nine of them in the patrol. They had been in the Zagros mountains for nearly a week. They had trudged along narrow stony paths. They had scrambled up steep, rough slopes. They had camped out in the open, shivering in sleeping-bags that never felt quite thick enough to keep out the cold. The SA80 rifles and Bergen packs they had to carry seemed to weigh a ton. Their bellies rumbled, because army rations never quite filled them up.

The soldiers felt as though they had been tramping through the mountains for months, not days. They had not yet seen any sign of the men they were hunting. They were starting to wonder if the men even existed. The only living beings the soldiers had seen, apart from each other, were a few wild goats. Once, they'd heard the cry of an eagle. They had looked up, but the bird had been hidden in the clouds. That cry was the most lonely sound in the world.

Now the patrol's leader, Captain Carr, ordered the men to take a rest. The soldiers dropped their Bergens and sat on them. They brewed some tea and shared out chocolate and cigarettes.

Carr drew Sergeant Dex Hammond aside for a quiet word.

"What's your view on this, sergeant?" Carr asked Hammond. "Wild goose chase or what?"

"The intelligence was pretty clear, sir," Hammond replied. He was Carr's second in command on this mission. "The rebels are holed up somewhere round here."

"Yes, but what do you think?" Carr said.

Hammond paused. "Satellite hasn't spotted anyone. But the rebels are locals. They know this region like the back of their hands. They know every nook and cranny. If they want to hide here, then they won't be seen. Not by satellites and most of all not by us. I expect they can hear us coming a mile off."

"You think we haven't a hope of finding them," said Carr.

"I'd say the chances were somewhere between slim and nil," said Hammond.

Carr gave a quick grin. "I've always admired you for being so frank, Hammond. And you're right. There's a saying in these parts. *The Kurds have no friends but the mountains.* And it's true. The mountains have always been a safe hiding place for them, most of all up here in the north. However ..."

Carr gave a shrug.

"We don't have much choice," he went on. "We have to keep looking. These rebels have become a right pain in the neck. The Kurds didn't even have a proper country until a few years ago, when Iraq was liberated. Now that they do, the rebels are trying hard to make it an Islamic state."

"But our leaders don't like that idea," said Hammond.

"The West wants a democratic Kurdistan, yes. One where the people choose their rulers, rather than God doing it."

"Because of all that uranium that's been found down in the south. Europe and America are keen to get their hands on it. That won't happen if Kurdistan goes Islamic."

The rebels were attacking anyone from the West, not just the troops, all across Kurdistan. They shot people from the mining companies, who were working on ways of getting the uranium out of the ground. They lobbed mortars into the British and American embassies. There had been suicide bombings in several towns and cities, including the new Kurdish capital, the city of Van. The Independent Republic of Kurdistan was in chaos, and British troops had been called in to help keep the peace. And to wipe out the rebels.

"We're soldiers, sergeant," said Captain Carr. "It's not up to us to ask why we have to do something. We just do it. So come on. Let's get going again."

He ordered the men to get back on their feet. The patrol marched onward.

An hour passed, and Hammond began to feel uneasy. The silence had grown deeper. The wind had dropped. The sleet still fell, like icy needles, but it was as though the mountains were holding their breath. Waiting for something to happen.

Hammond told himself that it was just because he was tired. His brain was fuzzy after a week without a proper night's sleep. He was starting to see things that weren't there.

But still he couldn't shake off the feeling that someone was watching the patrol.

He seemed to sense eyes peering down from the crags above. Someone was following the patrol's progress. Someone knew the soldiers were there, and was lying in wait for them.

Hammond should have said something about this to Captain Carr, but he knew what would happen if he did. Carr would laugh at him and tell him not to be foolish. The boss wasn't the kind of man who paid much attention to "funny feelings". He put his faith in things he could feel and touch. In that respect he was typical of anyone who had trained at Sandhurst. There, at the Royal Military Academy, they turned out officers who did everything by the book. But Hammond thought they also turned out officers who didn't have any common sense, or any instinct for danger.

Unless Hammond could prove that there was someone up there watching, Carr would never believe him. And Hammond couldn't prove it. He wasn't even 100% sure of it himself. He only had his gut to go on, and his gut was telling him that the rebels were hiding close by. The patrol was going to engage with the enemy very soon.

He gripped his rifle hard.

The soldiers reached the top of a sharp ridge. At their feet lay a long, V-shaped valley. Carr told one of the men, Private Andrews, to check their position with his GPS unit.

Andrews looked at the screen of his little hand-held device. He said, "Yep, I've managed to pinpoint where we are. If this is right, we're in the middle of fucking nowhere."

The others chuckled. Their laughter rolled down into the valley, with an echo like faint thunder.

"That's enough of that," said Carr, with a flicker of a smile. "Send a note of our position back to base. Then we head down that way." He pointed towards the bottom of the valley.

Hammond looked. It was very narrow down there. The steep sides of the valley were studded with rocks and thorny trees. The rocks were large enough for men to hide behind. The trees too.

"Sir, I'm not sure that's such a good idea," Hammond said to Carr.

Carr frowned. "What do you mean?"

"If you'll excuse me, the bottom of that valley is the perfect spot for an ambush. We should avoid it and go around the top."

"I hear what you say, Sergeant Hammond," said Carr. "However, down through the valley is the fastest route, not to mention the simplest. If we go around the top, it'll mean going an extra three or four kilometres."

"But sir, the extra distance doesn't matter," said Hammond. "It's not as if we're in a hurry to get somewhere. This is a search mission, not a race."

"True," said Carr. "So let's search through the valley. That's an order."

"But sir – "

"That's an order," said Carr again.

Hammond bit his lip. There was no point arguing. The boss had made up his mind. They would just have to live with it.

The patrol set off down into the valley, single file.

Hammond switched his SA80 from "safety" to triple-shot mode. Fear prickled through his body. He prayed that he was wrong. He prayed that his feeling of being watched was all in his mind.

But he couldn't help picturing the rebels in his mind. They were lying silent and still among the rocks and trees. They had AK-47s in their hands and the British soldiers in their sights. He saw their dusty, drab clothes and turbans, perfect cover in this kind of country. These were men who could merge with the mountains they lived in, vanishing into the landscape.

A bead of sweat trickled down his spine.

Then something exploded 20 metres away. A rocket-propelled grenade. It kicked up a shower of dirt and stone.

The patrol threw themselves to the ground, flat on their faces.

Bullets thwipped and bounced all around them.

Captain Carr shouted, "Engage! Engage! Return fire!"

The SA80s barked.

Another RPG landed, and someone screamed.

Hammond saw Private Andrews. Andrews was thrashing around on the ground. Half his face had been torn away. Blood poured from the ragged hole where his left eye should have been. Beside him another of the men was lying dead. His belly had burst open. A mass of mangled guts spilled out from the hole.

The SA80 leapt in Hammond's hands as he squeezed the trigger. He strafed the sides of the valley with bursts of gunfire. He couldn't see the enemy's positions. He shot without aiming. It felt as if he was fighting the very landscape itself.

The valley rumbled with the echo of the guns. The sleet was still falling, slow and white and steady. Above, the sky was a blank slate of grey.

The sounds faded into nothing. Hammond could no longer hear anything, not the soldiers screaming, not the rattle of gunfire.

It was like a dream.

It was a dream.

Hammond snapped awake. He was in bed. He was at home, in his flat in the mess. His radio alarm clock said 3:14AM. The numbers glowed red in the dark.

His heart was pounding. His skin was damp with sweat.

Hammond staggered to the bathroom and soaked his face in cold water. He went into the living room, which had a small kitchen, and made himself coffee. Then he turned on the TV and clicked it to the Discovery Channel. He knew that he wouldn't get back to sleep tonight. He never did when he had this dream. He watched a series of films about sharks for the rest of the night, until dawn broke.

Then he put on his kit and went to work.

Want *more?*

Dead Brigade

---

by

James Lovegrove

A new kind of soldier ...

This is the British Army of the future.
Soldiers brought back from the dead to
fight as robots.

The zombie army can learn.

They can kill.

The only thing they can't do is die.

Even if they want to ...